THE ALICE AND JERRY BASIC READERS

READING FOUNDATION PROGRAM

The New
Through the
Green Gate

by

MABEL O'DONNELL

Illustrated by
Florence and Margaret
Hoopes

ROW, PETERSON AND COMPANY

HOME OFFICE: EVANSTON, ILLINOIS

Contents

THROUGH THE GREEN GATE

BANG

1953 Edition

Copyright, **1948**, 1939. Row, Peterson and Company. 4214
Registered in U.S. Patent Office. Printed in the U.S.A.
International and Imperial Copyright secured.

PATCHES

TWO KINDS OF LUCK

Miss Lizzie

Someday you may go to Friendly Village. Of course, when you get there, you will want to see all your old friends, Alice and Jerry, Bobby and Billy, and Paddy and all his pets.

You will want to call on Mr. Carl and say "Hello" to Mr. Andrews in his fruit store on River Street.

Maybe Cobbler Jim will let you sit on the end of his workbench and talk to his old black cat while he mends your shoes.

But whatever you do, be sure to take a walk down Green Gate Road to see Miss Lizzie. You don't want to go home without seeing Miss Lizzie.

Green Gate Road runs right by the houses of Alice and Jerry and Mr. Carl, and out to the edge of the village. Then all at once it stops.

I suppose you think it stops because there is no more village and no place else to go. But that isn't it.

Green Gate Road has to stop because right there at the end of the road is a little stone house with two fat, red chimneys.

Around the house is a garden where gay-colored flowers grow in the summertime. Around the garden is a wall, and in the wall is a green gate. It is just the kind of gate that makes you want to look through the cracks to see what is happening on the other side.

No one in Friendly Village knows how old the house and the wall really are. But that isn't important. The important thing is that Miss Lizzie lives there.

Miss Lizzie's hair used to be yellow, but now it is turning gray. Most of the time she is dressed in blue because she likes blue and because that is the color of her eyes.

"She is little, but oh, my!" Mr. Carl likes to say. And that means that Miss Lizzie can do more work than any two people put together, and do it in no time at all. It means that when she is cross, she is very, very cross, and that when she is happy, she is happy all over.

On Sunday mornings Miss Lizzie puts on her best hat with the gay red roses and walks down the street to church. Then it looks as if she were no bigger than Alice and Jerry and the other boys and girls who are waiting for her.

But when she walks in again at the garden gate and takes off the hat with the gay red roses, then she grows up. Anyway, she is big enough to look over the garden wall.

Time and time again, Alice and Jerry and some of their friends stand outside the garden wall and call,

"Hurry, Miss Lizzie! Come as fast as you can! We have something to show you."

Then Miss Lizzie will look right over the wall with a smile on her face and a twinkle in her eye. She will try to make her voice sound cross, as she calls,

"Oh, dear me! What do you want now?"

Of course, if you want to be friends with Miss Lizzie, you will have to like Amber, too. Amber is Miss Lizzie's old yellow cat. The thing Amber likes best to do is to sleep in the sun on the old stone wall.

Because Miss Lizzie lives at the edge of the village, the cornfields of the country are right at her back door.

Whenever Jerry and his friends go to the woods, they have to walk by Miss Lizzie's door. On the way home they always stop to show her what they have found. Whatever they find—frog eggs, or tadpoles, or queer-looking spiders— they always give her a few.

Summer or winter, spring or fall, all the boys and girls come to see Miss Lizzie. They tell her all the exciting things that happen, and they tell her all their troubles.

Miss Lizzie smiles at all the exciting things, and she helps them out of all their troubles.

One day Jim Winters, who lives at White Fence Farm, was in great trouble. He didn't want anyone to know about it. But he had to have help from someone. So he went to Miss Lizzie.

I suppose you want to know what the trouble was all about. I suppose you want to know what Miss Lizzie told him to do. Your questions won't stop until I tell you. So here is what happened.

BANG

My Big Brother

Some boys like to talk about their dogs. Some boys like to talk about cowboys and Indians and things like that. But Jim Winters didn't. He liked to talk about his big brother.

The minute Jim moved to White Fence Farm, he started to talk about Joe.

White Fence Farm was on the way from Miss Lizzie's house to the Big Woods. As soon as Jerry and the other boys heard that someone new was coming to live there, they remembered that they had to go to the woods right away. So they started off on the run.

"Where to now?" asked Miss Lizzie, as she looked at them over the garden wall.

"To the woods! It's something important! We can't wait a minute!" called Jerry.

But when the boys got to White Fence Farm, the important thing was forgotten. They took their time and looked and looked to see who was moving in.

At last they saw what they were looking for. A skinny boy with long legs, who looked very much like any other boy!

"I'm Jim Winters, and I'm going to live here always," said the new boy, with a jolly grin. "Wait until you see my big brother. He can play ball better than anyone in your town. Every time he plays, he makes a home run."

"Oh, you are just talking!" said Jerry. "There are a hundred ball players in this town, and any one of them is better than your brother."

"You just wait and see!" said Jim. "In the town we came from, Joe played football. He was the fullback and the captain, too."

"Oh, he was not! I don't believe it!" said Paddy. "Show me your big brother!"

"All right, I will!" said Jim. "I'm not afraid. Joe is out on his pony now, and I tell you it is a wild pony, too."

"Oh, it is not! Your father would not have a wild pony on his farm," said Bobby.

"Just you wait and see!" called Jim, as he started off to find Joe. "Follow me, but you had better get out of the way when that pony bucks."

All the boys followed Jim on the run. When they came to the south pasture, there were Joe and the pony. The pony was grazing away while Joe mended the fence.

"Hello, fellows! Where did you come from?" asked Joe, when the boys came nearer. "Any fence menders among you?"

Something in Joe's jolly smile, and the way he called them "fellows," made Jerry and the other boys think that maybe Jim was right, after all. Maybe Joe was as great as Jim thought he was.

And oh, that pony! He was brown and white. His coat was as smooth and shining as could be. He had a beautiful tail. Maybe it was no longer than any other pony's tail, but it looked longer.

He was friendly enough while he was eating grass. But when Joe called, "Here, Bang! Here, Old Fellow!" the boys saw that he could be another kind of pony when he wanted to be.

Bang looked like a wild pony now. There was fire in his brown eyes as he walked up to Joe. His ears were flat back on his head. He was doing his best to look mean.

Joe laughed in his big jolly way.

"You old rascal!" he said. "You are just trying to show off. You want the boys to think you are wild. But you are not wild, and I know it."

Then Joe gave Bang a good hard slap.

"Stop it, Bang! Stop it!" he said. "I mean what I say, Old Fellow!"

In a minute the fire was gone from the pony's eyes. Up went his ears, and he looked as if he could never be mean, not even if he wanted to be.

"The only time Bang makes trouble is when he thinks he can get his own way," said Joe, as he turned to the boys.

"Make him buck, Joe! Please!" cried Jim. "I told the boys he would, but they would not believe me."

"Would not believe you! Well, I declare!" said Joe. "Come on, Bang! Show them what a bucking pony can do. Get back out of the way, boys, and hurry up about it, too."

Joe jumped onto the pony's back and started him on a trot across the pasture.

For a time, all went well. Jerry was just going to say, "He isn't a bucking pony, after all. Anyone can ride him!" when bang! Down went the pony's head, and out went his back legs. That pony bucked! Oh, how he did buck!

"See! I told you! That is how it happens! With a bang! That is why Joe calls him Bang!" shouted Jim.

"Do it again! Do it again!" shouted all the boys together.

So Joe did it again and then again. The boys wished that he would never stop. But Bang was Joe's pony, and Joe knew the very minute Bang began to grow tired.

"Enough for today!" said Joe, as he jumped down from the pony's back. He stood with his arm around the pony's neck and talked to the boys.

"What makes him buck?" asked Jerry.

"Just because I want him to!" answered Joe. "He learned how early last spring. You see, Jerry, I give him the sign. He won't buck for everyone. Just for me!"

"Sign? Sign, did you say? What sign? Oh, come on, Joe! Tell me what it is!" said one boy and then another.

"Oh, NO!" said Joe. "The first thing I know, some of you fellows will be trying it out. Bang knows the sign, and I know. But no one else will ever know until he finds it out for himself."

"And now let me tell you something, boys," Joe went on. "Keep away from this pony. Remember that! Don't let me catch you trying to ride him. Do you understand?"

And just from the way Joe said it, the boys understood.

In the days and weeks that followed, all that the boys could talk about was Joe and the bucking pony.

And the sign! The boys never gave up trying to find out about that. Every time Bang bucked, they thought they had it. But they didn't.

"What do you want to know for, anyway?" asked Joe, with a smile on his face and a twinkle in his eye. "Bang knows, and I know, but we are not telling."

So there it ended.

An Early Morning Surprise

Weeks went by. Winter came, and the boys had great fun coasting downhill on their sleds. After winter, spring came, then summer, and Joe was going away.

"He is going out West on a ranch. Out where Indians live in hogans! He is going to corral cattle out on the range," Jim told Jerry. The news went like wildfire from one boy to another.

"He will be the best cowboy out West," they all said. And they really believed it.

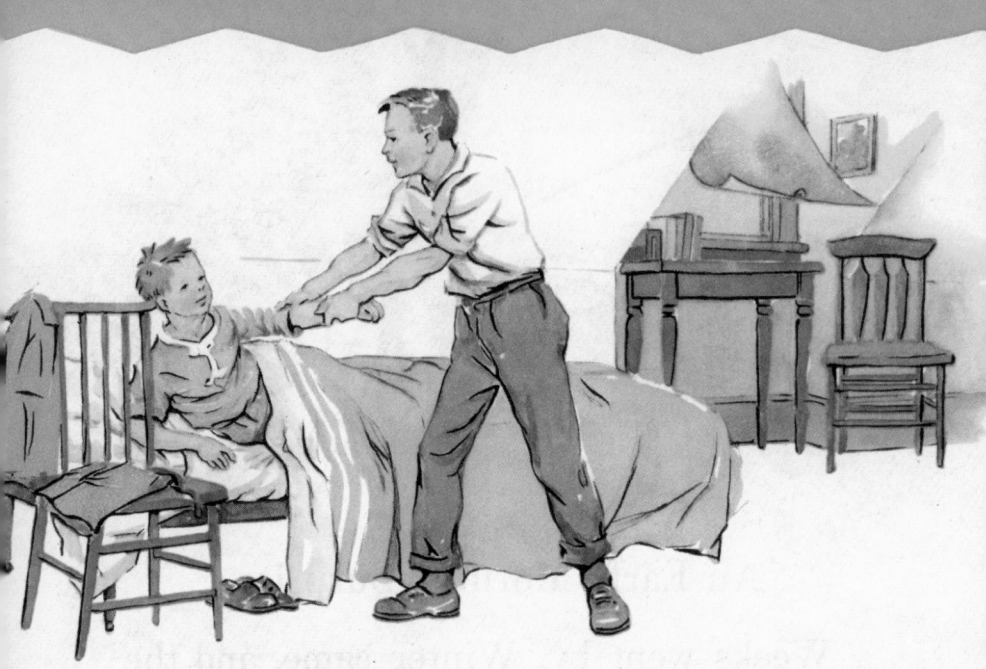

The morning before Joe went away, he pulled Jim out of bed before it was even light. The sun was just coming up.

"Are you ready for a surprise so early in the morning?" he asked with a jolly grin. "Come to the barn with me before the cows moo and want to be milked."

The minute they got to the barn, Joe gave Bang his breakfast. While the pony was eating, Joe talked to Jim.

"I would not give Bang to anyone else, Jim, but I'm giving him to you," said Joe. "I will be gone for weeks and weeks. Anyway, my legs are too long for that pony right now. You have been going for the cows on Old Betsy for almost a year. You know how to ride horseback. From now on, Bang is your pony. I will show you how to put on his saddle, and I will watch you take your first ride."

Now, I suppose you think Jim was happy, so happy that he gave a shout and threw his cap into the air. That isn't the way it was at all.

The very minute Joe said, "From now on, Bang is your pony," a queer feeling came over Jim. He didn't want that feeling. He wished it would go away.

But the feeling didn't go away. There it was, big and deep down inside of Jim. It was growing bigger every minute. He was afraid of Bang, and he never wanted to ride him, no, never!

When your brother gives you a pony, the pony that he thinks is the best in the world, you must say something. Jim wanted to thank Joe, but he couldn't. The feeling wouldn't let him.

"Do Father and Mother know about it?" he asked at last. "Do they think that it is all right for me to have Bang?"

All the time he was talking, he was thinking, "I hope Father thinks that Bang is too wild. I hope that Mother will not let me have him."

But things didn't turn out that way.

"Oh, yes," said Joe. "We talked it over last night. They know that you have been waiting and waiting until you were old enough to ride Bang. They are delighted that you are going to have him."

By this time Bang was through with his breakfast.

"See here, Old Fellow," said Joe, as he started to put on the saddle. "From now on, you are Jim's pony. Take good care of him, Bang, until I get back."

As long as Joe was going to watch him ride, there was nothing else for Jim to do but hop onto the pony's back. He would not have Joe know that he was afraid, not if he could help it.

"Will he buck, Joe?" asked Jim, as he was climbing into the saddle. His voice shook, and his arms and legs shook, too.

"Is that the trouble?" said Joe. "Forget about that from this minute on, Jim. Bang won't buck without the sign, and no one knows that but me. I would not let you ride him if it were not safe. You believe me, don't you?"

After that Jim began to feel better. He didn't enjoy the ride, but he knew that he didn't have to be afraid with Joe around. He headed Bang on a trot up and down the pasture so that Joe could see him.

"Fine!" said Joe, when the ride was over. "You're a smart boy, Jim."

The next day Joe went away.

"If you want any help," he said, as he bought a ticket to ride on the train, "go to Jack." Jack was the man who worked for Jim's father.

"Jack showed me how to ride when I began," Joe went on. "And don't forget! Bang won't buck! He is the best pony in the world, and by the time I get back, you will think so, too."

But Jim knew that he would not.

Bang Gets His Own Way

All Jim could think about the next morning was, "I have to ride Bang. If I don't, Joe will think I am no good at all. All I will be is his little brother."

The morning was almost over when at last he went out to the barn to find Jack.

All the time the saddle was being fastened, Bang's two brown eyes looked at Jim.

"I wish he would not look at me like that," thought Jim. "He looks so mean."

When Jim climbed onto Bang's back, his legs shook against the saddle. His hands holding the lines shook, too. If only Joe were here to tell him what to do! Then he would not be afraid.

Bang started off at a trot. Jim wanted to ride down to the road that went to Friendly Village and then turn around again. But Bang headed for the north pasture, and Jim did not try to stop him.

As they went through the pasture gate, Bang started to eat the long grass. A pony was not supposed to do that, not with someone on his back. The thing to do was to give Bang a slap and send him on his way. But Jim could not do that.

"What if he bucked?" thought Jim, and because the lines shook, Bang knew that his rider was afraid.

Bang walked around the pasture until he had all the grass he could eat. Then he headed for the barn and began to trot.

"Hold on there, hold on!" cried Jim. But the pony trotted faster and faster.

As Jim and the pony came to the pasture gate, Bang started to run. Jim pulled on the lines, but it did no good. Then he forgot everything that Joe had told him to do. All he could think of was how afraid he was.

By this time Jim was holding on to the saddle. He was not even trying to stop Bang any more. The pony was going faster and faster every minute.

All at once Bang turned to one side. Before Jim was quite sure what had happened, he was out of the saddle and on the grass. He looked up just in time to see Bang going in at the barn door.

As Jim picked himself up and walked to the barn, he could hear Jack whistle.

"I—I fell off!" said Jim.

Jack went right on with his work. "That is what I thought," he said.

"I—I didn't get hurt!" Jim went on.

Jack did not look up from his work. "I thought you would be all right. Bang let Joe off, too, without hurting him."

"Do you mean—do you mean that Joe fell off when he first learned to ride?" asked Jim. He could not believe his ears.

"That is what I mean. But Joe got right back on again. He let Bang know that he could not get his own way," said Jack.

Jim turned red. He knew that Jack expected him to get back on the pony. He looked around for Bang. There he was, as mean-looking as ever. No, Jack couldn't make him ride Bang again. Not even Joe could make him do that. Next time he might get hurt, really hurt.

Jack did not even look up as Jim whistled and walked away.

But Jim had not gone far when he heard Jack say, "Jim is not like Joe, Bang. Jim gives up."

Lazy Days

Later that same afternoon Jim went for the cows on Old Betsy.

Again he heard Jack talking to Bang. "Jim is not like Joe, Bang. He rides an old horse and leaves you in the barn."

Days went by, and Jim did not go near the pony. For a day or two Father asked, "Did you ride Bang today?" When Jim always answered "No," Father gave up and asked no longer. But from the way Father looked at him, Jim had the feeling that Father knew what the trouble was.

"He thinks I'm afraid! He thinks I'm no good!" thought Jim. But even that did not make him want to ride Bang.

Then one day Jim went to the barn, and Bang was not there. Jim did not want to say anything, but the words just came out.

"Where is Bang?" he asked Jack.

"Well, he isn't big enough to carry your father or mother," said Jack. "I can't be fiddling around taking care of him. So I turned him out to pasture."

All through the hot summer days that followed, Bang had a fine time. He ran when he pleased. He ate grass when he pleased. He rolled over and over when he pleased. He even went to sleep when he pleased. And he grew fat and lazy.

Many a time Jim and Jerry and the other boys stood by the fenced-in pasture to watch Bang grazing. Jim did not tell the boys that Bang was his pony. He would not have them find that out for anything.

Then one morning the postman gave Jim a letter, a letter from Joe. In four weeks Joe would be home. If Jim could ride well enough—and Joe knew that he could—Joe might show him the sign. So Jim was to say "Hello" to Bang for Joe, and ride and ride and ride.

Jim did not show that letter to anyone, not even to Mother. He put it into his pocket. Every time he was alone, he pulled it out and looked at it once more. Every time he opened it, he wished that he could ride Bang. Oh, how he wished that he could ride Bang! Only four weeks! What was he going to do?

When he could stand it no longer, he went to see Miss Lizzie.

Miss Lizzie liked to bake, and this morning she was doing what she liked to do. She was baking. Her kitchen was full of good smells. They came out of the door and over the garden and through the green gate.

But do you know? When Jim came in at the green gate, he didn't smell a smell. All he could think of was Bang.

"What is the trouble now?" asked Miss Lizzie, as she turned to put the milk on the ice. "You look as if you didn't have a friend left in the world."

Before long the warm smells of the kitchen, Miss Lizzie's happy smile, and a big piece of cake made Jim feel better.

"Miss Lizzie," he asked, "what would you do if someone gave you a pony?"

"My stars!" said Miss Lizzie. "I would give him right back again. What would I do with a pony?"

Then, as Miss Lizzie turned to put the cake away, she had a thought, and the thought made her say,

"Of course, if I were you, Jim, I would keep the pony, and every day I would tell myself how lucky I was."

"Yes, but what if he had a mean look? What would you do then?" Jim went on.

"Well, maybe I would have a mean look myself," said Miss Lizzie. "I would not let any pony get the better of me."

"Yes, but what if he bucked!" said Jim.

"Well, don't talk in riddles," said Miss Lizzie. "If it is a bucking pony you are riddling about, you may have a hard time. What is the trouble, anyway?"

When Miss Lizzie heard all there was to tell, she said, "Things are not so bad as they might be. If Jack could make a rider out of Joe, he can make one out of you. Take this letter to him. Tell him that you are afraid of Bang, but that you will ride him anyway. Then do what Jack tells you to do. You have only four weeks."

"He always keeps saying I'm not like Joe," said Jim, looking at the floor.

"Well, he is right," said Miss Lizzie. "You won't be like Joe until you can ride Bang. So run along and get started."

Bang Can't Get His Own Way

"So Joe is coming home," said Jack with a smile so big that it went from ear to ear. "We can't let him find a fat, lazy pony eating grass in a pasture, can we, Jim?"

"Certainly I will help you," Jack went on. "I would have helped you all along if you had only asked. Joe told me not to make you ride that pony until you really wanted to. And you never really wanted to until today. I will ride him myself for a day or two until he is broken in again. Then he will be ready for you. Come to think of it, I will put away my shovel and go after him right now. His lazy days are over."

For the next two days Jack was the one who rode Bang. Every minute he could take from his work, he was on the pony's back. Poor Bang had such a workout that he was all tired out.

All the time Jack was at work in the barn, he was talking to Jim. And Jim listened to every word.

"Never let an animal know that you are afraid of him," said Jack. "The very minute you do, he will try to get his own way. Joe told you that Bang would not buck, and you didn't believe him. What happened was all your own doings."

Now the two days were over, and it was time for Jim to ride Bang once more.

As he climbed into the saddle, he was thinking over and over to himself, "Joe told me this pony was safe. He told me that Bang would not buck. Joe knows."

Jim was thinking so hard about Joe and what he had said that he forgot to think about being afraid. So he was not afraid. And Bang guessed that, too.

Bang started to head for the north pasture. He remembered the last time Jim was on his back. Maybe he could get his own way again.

"Oh, no you don't!" said Jim, as he pulled on the lines to turn the pony's head. "We are going a little way down the road to Friendly Village, Mr. Bang. Don't you forget that."

And down the road they went. Bang gave up. He saw that he could not get his own way from now on. So he gave up trying.

From that morning on, Jim was on Bang's back almost every minute of the day.

Every night when he brought Bang into the barn, he stopped and said to Jack,

"Am I as good a rider as Joe?"

And Jack always answered with a smile that went from ear to ear, "Not by a long ways! But you are coming!"

And even that made Jim very happy.

Jim had never been so proud before as he was on the day when he rode into Friendly Village on Bang's back.

Of course, he stopped to see Miss Lizzie on the way. She had her rake and was working among her roses. Amber was enjoying the sun on the old stone wall.

All at once Amber gave a big jump right down onto Miss Lizzie's shoulder.

"My stars! I'm not surprised you jumped," cried Miss Lizzie, as she looked around. There was a pony's head coming right in over the garden wall.

"Come out and see Bang!" called Jim.

"I'm coming! I'm coming!" called Miss Lizzie. "But keep him out of my garden. Don't you bring him in here."

And out went Miss Lizzie in a hurry.

"Wait until your big brother sees you," was all Miss Lizzie could say, as she looked up at Jim with shining eyes.

Then she put her hand down into her big pocket, and out came a red apple for Bang. From that minute on, Bang was like everyone else in Friendly Village. He liked Miss Lizzie, too.

In the next few minutes the news went like wildfire all over the village.

"Here comes Jim! He can ride Bang! Come and see! Come and see!"

All the boys and girls in the village came on the run. Oh, such a crowd!

When they heard that Bang was really Jim's pony, they all began to shout at once, "Let me ride him! Oh, come on, Jim! You know me!"

But Jim just looked down at them from the pony's back and said,

"You will have to try Old Betsy first. You don't think you can ride a wild pony like Bang the very first thing, do you?"

"I guess not," said one boy and then another. From that minute on, they thought Jim was a great fellow.

Surprises Never End

The days went slowly by, one by one. Eight, seven, six, five! Five more days, and then Joe would be home.

One morning Jim was riding Bang through the Big Woods. It was a lovely day in early autumn. As Jim rode along, he watched the red and yellow leaves as they fell from the trees.

All at once a cottontail rabbit ran out from under some leaves. Bang would step on the rabbit. Jim knew that he would. Without thinking what he was doing, he pulled on the lines and began to dig into Bang's side with his left knee.

Then something happened. Jim never could tell how it happened. But it did.

Down went Bang's head and out went his back legs. Bang bucked!

For a minute Jim thought he could never stay on that pony's back, but he did. He had a good hold on the lines, and he went on holding to the saddle with his knees as hard as he could. In another minute Bang was walking along as if nothing had happened.

Jim was so surprised that he could hardly sit in the saddle. Had Bang really bucked? If he had, it was not so bad, after all. But what had made him buck? The rabbit? Was that it? The rabbit was not a sign, and Joe said that Bang would not buck without the sign. Then Jim remembered his knee. Could that be it? Oh, oh, oh! Suppose he had found the sign!

I suppose you think that Jim went dashing back to the barn to tell Jack all about it. Well, he didn't. There was only one thought in his head.

"I must try it! I must try it!" he thought, and he did try it. He pulled on the lines and began to dig into Bang's side with his left knee. Again Bang bucked. And this time there was nothing to be afraid of at all. Jim really enjoyed it.

"I have it!" he cried at the top of his voice. "Wait until Jack hears about this."

"I have it!" he called several more times, without stopping to remember that there was no one around to hear him call.

Jim stayed in the woods for the rest of the morning. When he rode into the barnyard, he was shouting at the top of his voice for Jack to come and see.

Then right in front of the barn door where Jack was standing, Jim made Bang buck.

"Upon my word! I never thought you could do it!" shouted Jack. He threw his hat into the air, and it flew away up on the shingles of the barn roof.

"Am I as good a rider as Joe now?" asked Jim.

"You are almost!" said Jack, and the smile on his face went from ear to ear.

Now Jim thought the days would never
go by. But they did. Four, three, two,
one! This very day Joe was coming home.

Maybe there were cowboys, and Indians
in hogans, and special things like these
out West. But Jim had something to show
Joe, too. Jack and Jim had it all worked
out. They had put their heads together
and thought how they could give Joe the
biggest surprise he had ever had.

Jim was going to ride Bang down to
the train. Jack would keep the people out
of the way so that no one would get hurt.
Yes, they had it all worked out.

When the train pulled in, there was Joe at the top of the steps, all ready to hop off. He jumped down and said "Hello" to Father. Then he turned to give Mother a big, big hug.

Then all at once, in the street behind them, he saw Jim on Bang's back.

"Howdy, Jim! Howdy, Bang, good old fellow!" he cried, as he started for them on the run.

"Keep out of the way, Joe, and hurry up about it, too," called Jim.

And then, right in front of Joe's eyes, with all the people looking on, Bang bucked.

For a minute Joe stood still with his mouth open, too surprised to say a word.

"You rascals!" he called, as he ran over to Jim and the pony. He stood with one arm around Jim and one around the pony's neck. "You rascals! Did Bang tell you the sign, Jim? How did you find out?"

"I found it out for myself," said Jim.

"And what do you think of Bang now?" Joe asked next.

"I am so glad he is my pony," said Jim. "He is the best pony in the world."

Then Joe smiled his own jolly smile. "Of course he is, big brother," said Joe. "Bang is the best pony in the world."

PATCHES

Wanted, a Dog

As long as Billy Gray could remember, he had wanted a dog. Billy was eight years old, but he liked to say that he was going on nine. That made him feel so much older. Now that you know how old Billy was, you know that he had been wanting a dog for a long, long time.

Billy didn't care very much what kind of dog it was. It could be a full-grown dog or only a puppy. It could be a bird dog, or a sheep dog, or a watchdog. It could be black or white, yellow or brown, skinny or fat. Any kind of dog would do, just so he could call it his own.

I suppose you are surprised to know that a boy could live to be eight, going on nine, without ever having owned a dog. Why didn't someone give him a dog? Why didn't some old dog follow him home? Why didn't he open the door some morning and find one on the doorstep? Other boys got all the dogs they wanted in ways like these.

You will be surprised to hear that all these things happened to Billy. They really did. Every one of them happened.

One birthday his grandmother on his mother's side gave him a dog, and his grandfather on his father's side gave him another.

Once Mr. Carl's brother Charlie had a dog that he did not want. So he said that Billy could have the dog.

Another time a poor old dog came to Friendly Village. No one could find out where he came from. The poor old dog followed Billy home.

One cold night Billy heard something at the door. He opened the door in a hurry. There in the snow on the doorstep was a wee little puppy that tried to jump on Billy and lick his hand.

So, you see, it is just as I told you. All the things that might have happened to give Billy a dog, really happened. But still he didn't have a dog.

The trouble was that the dogs never stayed long enough for Billy to feel that they were his own. They had bread and milk and a bone or two. They stayed until they got over being tired and hungry.

But by that time Mother found dog tracks on the steps, and dog hair on her clean kitchen floor. Then she began to get all worked up. That means that she began to think of all the bad things that might happen with a dog around.

Mother thought what the neighbors would say when a dog ran after their baby ducks or raced through their garden. A dog might snap at some little girl, or even at Billy himself. A dog was sure to be run over by some car. And if the family wanted to go away, what in the world could be done with a dog while they were away?

Mother thought about the bad things, but she forgot the good. She forgot how nice it is to come home and find someone there who is happy to see you. She forgot the good feeling you have when your dog jumps up on you and wags and wags and wags his tail until he is just one big wag all over. She forgot how much a boy can like a dog, and a dog can like a boy.

And because Mother remembered the bad things and forgot the good, she always said something like this:

"Yes, Billy, I know you would like to keep this dog. But a dog around the house is so much trouble. You remember that new bicycle you wanted. Suppose we buy you the bicycle and forget about the dog."

Then Father and Mother would talk things over, and Father would always remember a man who lived away out in the country and wanted a dog. The man would get the dog, and Billy would get the bicycle or a cowboy suit or some toy he wanted. Other boys thought that the bicycle and the cowboy suit were the finest things in the world. But poor Billy still wished that he had a dog.

One More Dog

Late one afternoon just about supper-time, Mother asked Billy to take a basket of good things to eat to Mrs. Banks, who lived at the edge of town.

It looked very much like rain, and Mother told Billy to hurry.

There was a train standing on the track behind Mrs. Banks's house. Just as Billy started up the front walk, a dog ran out from under the wheels of the bunk car and stood looking at him.

Billy had never seen such a dog. He was old and so skinny that almost every one of his bones showed. His feet were too big, and his tail was too long. The long hair of his yellow coat was coming out in patches.

It was easy to see that Billy did not think much of this dog. He gave him just one look and went on into the house.

No sooner was he inside the door of the house than it began to rain. Of course, he had to wait until the rain was over.

It was evening when Billy started for home, and it was growing dark. This made him hurry faster than ever.

All at once something wet bumped against him. Something wet jumped up on him. It was that dog.

"You are a good dog," said Billy, as they ran along through the puddles together. "But you can't come into our house. If you stay on the steps, maybe I can bring you something to eat."

The dog looked as if he understood everything that Billy said to him. But when Billy opened the back door just a crack to get in himself, the dog didn't stay on the steps. Oh, no, he didn't do that. He put his two feet in the crack, and in another minute there was a dog in the middle of the kitchen floor.

Then what do you think that dog did? He shook himself. He splashed water all over Mother. He splashed water all over the food on the table. He splashed water all over everything.

"Oh-h-h-h-h-h!" cried Mother, and Father came on the run.

"BILLY GRAY! I declare! Will you never stop bringing home dogs! Get him out of here! Get him out of here!" cried Mother.

Sometimes things are so bad that they stop being bad, and you can't help but see the funny side. Mother expected Father to be cross—very cross. But when Father saw that dog with his too-big feet and his too-long tail, his yellow hair coming out in patches, and his bones all showing, Father just shouted.

"Hello, Patches! What kind of animal are you, anyway? Are you sure you are a dog?" said Father, and he laughed until he hurt all over.

It was too bad, but Mother would not join in the fun. She was cross at Father because he laughed. She didn't think the dog was a joke, and she didn't say a word about buying Billy the horn he wanted if he would forget about the dog.

"Get that dog out of here and get him out in a hurry!" was all she would say.

As long as Mother was going to keep on being cross, Patches had to go. Father and Billy knew that.

When Father got the poor old dog to the door, Billy saw that it was raining again.

"Oh, dear! He is wet now! And tired and cold and hungry! We can't put him out in the rain. We can't do that," said Billy.

"I will tell you what we can do," said Father. "We can put him in the cellar for the night." I think Father was sorry for that dog, too.

So Father opened the cellar door, and down went Patches.

"I wish I knew what to do with you in the morning," said Father, as he stood on the top step and looked down. "This time we cannot even give you away. No one in America wants a dog like you."

But what did Patches care about tomorrow? Before long he had a good supper and an old coat of Billy's to sleep on. What more could a dog want? Patches went to sleep and was happy.

The next morning when Billy got out of bed, the dog was gone.

"I gave him his breakfast and let him go," said Father. "Now see to it, Billy, that he stays away from here. If you don't, you are in for trouble."

Wanted, a Watchdog

That same morning Billy started up Green Gate Road to find Jerry. Billy wanted to play ball. On the way he saw something yellow running around in Mr. Hill's garden. Maybe it was Patches.

"That dog must not see me," thought Billy. So he turned around and went the other way.

The other way took him down Green Gate Road to Miss Lizzie's garden. He looked through the cracks of the gate to see what was happening on the other side.

Miss Lizzie was on her knees, digging around her roses and singing a tune.

"That is a nice song," said Billy, as he opened the gate and walked in.

"Do you think so?" asked Miss Lizzie, and she went right on working. "It is about a dog. I sang that song when I was a girl. I have been thinking about dogs all morning. I guess that is why that old song ran through my head."

"Why have you been thinking about dogs?" asked Billy.

"Because I think I will have to have one," said Miss Lizzie.

"Have to have a dog?" asked Billy. He couldn't believe that Miss Lizzie had really said that.

"Yes," said Miss Lizzie. "I heard something in my garden last night. Even in Friendly Village it isn't safe for an old lady like me to live alone without a watchdog. I have been thinking about getting a dog for a long time. But I never get around to do it."

"What kind of dog do you want?" Billy asked next.

"An old one!" said Miss Lizzie. "One that won't run Amber up a tree!"

"Do you want a good-looking dog?" Billy went on.

"I don't care how he looks, just so he won't snap at anyone and will watch the house at night," said Miss Lizzie.

"Maybe I know where you can get one," said Billy. "His name is Patches. He is a good dog. Honest he is! No fooling!"

"Well, bring him around and let me look him over," said Miss Lizzie. "I don't say that I will keep him, but I will see."

Before Miss Lizzie could say another word, Billy was out of the gate.

"Patches! Patches!" called Billy, as he ran down the street. He did not stop to think that the dog did not know that Father had named him Patches.

At last Billy saw Patches smelling around in front of Mr. Stone's bakeshop.

I guess the dog remembered his breakfast and his good supper of the night before. He wagged his tail and followed Billy down the street. Mrs. Bell, giving Penny a ride in her stroller, saw them and laughed and laughed.

I wish you could have been there to see Miss Lizzie when she saw that dog.

"Patches! And you call that a dog!" was all she could say. I am sure she would have put him out of the gate in a hurry if it had not been for Amber.

Amber was asleep in the sun on the old stone wall. When she heard Miss Lizzie's surprised voice, she stood up.

For a minute she stood ready to run up a tree if Patches jumped at her. But he didn't. He gave one bow-wow and stopped. There was a little wag to his tail. Not much, but a little.

Amber took one good look at him. "Mew," she said, and went back to sleep.

"Amber isn't afraid of him. He can stay," said Miss Lizzie.

Turkey Tails

In the days that followed, everyone in Friendly Village came to see Miss Lizzie's dog. And oh, the things that were said about him.

"Don't you care, Miss Lizzie," said Billy. "He is a good dog."

"Of course he is," said Miss Lizzie. "Wait a few weeks, and you will see."

And Miss Lizzie was right. It was surprising to see how good-looking Patches turned out to be.

Miss Lizzie cleaned Patches, and his rusty yellow hair fell out no longer. She gave him enough to eat, and he got some fat on his bones. Then his legs and tail didn't look so long, and his feet didn't look so big.

And he watched Miss Lizzie's house. He certainly did. He went to sleep right in front of the green gate. Nothing could happen with Patches around.

"He sleeps with one eye and one ear open," said Miss Lizzie, and I really believe he did.

Every day Billy came to see the dog.

"I'm so glad I found you, Patches," he would say. "Isn't he getting to be beautiful, Miss Lizzie? Isn't he?"

"Oh, I couldn't say that," said Miss Lizzie. "No, Billy, I couldn't say that."

And then, just when everything was going along so well, Patches got into trouble. That is, it looked as if he did.

One morning Alice and Jerry and Billy were going to bring stones up from the pasture for Miss Lizzie's rock garden.

Off they started down Green Gate Road from Jerry's house with a wagon bumping along behind them.

They liked to work, and they were as happy as most people are when they are doing something for someone they like very much.

But what was this they heard when they went in at the green gate? Such a cross voice shouting at poor Miss Lizzie!

"I am as sure as I stand here, lady, that your dog has been after my turkeys. I saw him in my turnip patch. And this isn't the first time. My old hen turkey has started to nest three times, and that dog of yours has broken up her nest every time. He ate the eggs, too."

The farmer was so cross that he must have thought that Miss Lizzie could not hear very well. He leaned over her and just shouted.

But Miss Lizzie was not afraid of any farmer. She shook her head faster and faster.

"Don't be silly!" she said. "It must be some other dog. Hens can cluck, ducks can quack, and roosters can cock-a-doodle-doo right in my garden, and Patches is too lazy to run after them. It wasn't my dog. Don't snap at me."

Miss Lizzie put her hand down on the dog's yellow head. Patches looked up at her as if he were trying to understand what the man was saying about him.

At last the farmer went off. He was still talking as he went through the gate.

When he had gone, Miss Lizzie turned to Alice and Jerry and Billy.

"Patches never went near his turkeys. Never!" she said. "Now, what are you three up to this morning?"

"We are going to bring stones for your rock garden," said Jerry. "Do you suppose Patches will pull the wagon and help out a little?"

Now, sometimes Patches was very willing to work and pulled the wagon without any trouble. But sometimes he would sit right down in the middle of the road and not move a step.

It was lucky for Patches that this was a day when he wanted to work.

In a few minutes Patches was tied to the wagon. When he got to the pasture, he waited while Alice and Jerry and Billy put the stones into the wagon.

Then up the hill to Miss Lizzie's house they went. Jerry was pulling, too, and Alice and Billy were helping at the back of the wagon.

A rock garden takes many more stones than you think. Alice and Jerry and Billy and Patches went on bringing one wagon full and then another. At last Miss Lizzie came out and asked if they were hungry. She was such a good cook, and she had a big piece of cake for each of them.

Patches looked as if he were too tired to move. He stood tied to the wagon with his mouth open.

"Yes, Miss Lizzie, we are through now," said Billy. "And I, for one, am hungry enough to eat Amber."

Just then, right through the green gate, came the farmer. He was crosser than ever. In his hand he waved some tail feathers—turkey tail feathers.

"That dog of yours has been at it again. And this time he got the old turkey and pulled out her tail feathers!" he shouted.

Miss Lizzie just stood and looked at him. Then the farmer stopped shouting. He looked at Patches tied to the wagon. He looked at the stones.

"Do you mean to tell me that your dog has been pulling that wagon all morning? I declare, I saw him running through my garden just as I was climbing down my ladder. I ran after him just in time to see the tail feathers fly. I can't believe that he has been pulling that wagon. I just can't believe it."

"Well," said Billy. "You will have to believe it. We tied Patches to the wagon just after you left. He has worked hard all morning. Haven't you, Old Fellow?"

"I told you it was some other dog," said Miss Lizzie. "There are yellow dogs in the village and yellow dogs on farms. But my dog didn't run after the turkeys."

The farmer did not say another word. He turned and went out of the gate. But before many minutes he was back again.

"I am sorry, lady," he said. "I was so sure it was your dog. I hope you will believe me. I will tell you what I will do. Let me send you a nice turkey all dressed and ready for the pan. I want you to know that I am sorry for shouting at a lady and talking so about her dog."

So now you know how Patches almost got into trouble but didn't, and why Miss Lizzie had turkey for dinner even when it was not Thanksgiving.

An Old Dog, an Old Trick

One day not long after Patches had helped with the rock garden, Billy thought of something. He remembered how Jim Winters' pony, Bang, had learned to buck. Billy thought that he would teach Patches some tricks.

Billy was proud of himself for having thought of teaching tricks to Patches, until he talked to Miss Lizzie.

"Why, Billy. I am surprised at you," said Miss Lizzie. "Haven't you heard that you can't teach an old dog new tricks? That dog couldn't learn a new trick if he tried forever. Find a better way of spending your time."

But Billy thought he would try anyway. Patches might surprise Miss Lizzie.

First Billy tried the "sit up" trick. Patches was too old to sit up. He would fall over every time and then get up and wag his tail. He thought that Billy was joking and having fun with him.

Next Billy tried the "carry a basket" trick. Then he tried the "walk on your back legs" trick, and the "talk for your supper" trick. But it was of no use. Miss Lizzie was right. You can't teach an old dog new tricks, and Patches proved it.

Then one day Billy and Patches were walking along the riverbank together. Billy wanted to go fishing, and he was looking for worms.

Billy picked up a stick and threw it into the water to see how fast it would go. Before he knew what had happened, Patches had jumped into the water. The dog went after the stick and brought it back to Billy.

Billy stood there with his mouth open. He could hardly believe his eyes. Patches was still holding the stick.

"Did this just happen," thought Billy, "or can it be that Patches really knows a trick?"

He tried it again. He threw the stick as far out into the water as he could.

"Get it, Patches, get it!" he cried. Patches was in the water before he had started talking. Again the dog got the stick and brought it back to Billy.

"Patches!" cried Billy, and he put his arms around the wet dog's neck. "You know a trick. You know a great trick. It is better than all the 'sit up' tricks in the world."

Billy was so pleased with Patches that Patches was pleased with himself. He ran around and wagged his tail until it looked as if it would wag off.

Of course, Billy could not wait to tell Miss Lizzie. He went racing up the road, and you know who raced with him.

When Billy and Patches got to the gate, they were going so fast that they could not stop. So Patches jumped over the gate, and Billy did, too.

Miss Lizzie was taking a nap, but Billy went on calling, "Miss Lizzie!" until she had to get out of bed to stop him.

"You and that dog!" she said, as she leaned out of the window. Her face was red, and she was just as cross as anyone else is who has to get up before a nap is over.

No, she didn't think Patches was the smartest dog in the world because he went into the river after an old stick.

No, Miss Lizzie would not go down to the river to see a good-for-nothing dog do a silly trick like that. And that was the end of it.

When anyone is as cross as Miss Lizzie was, the only thing to do is to get out of the way as fast as you can.

"Don't you care, Patches," said Billy, as he started out of the gate on the run. "I will get my fishline, and we will go straight back to the river. I will watch you do your trick, even if Miss Lizzie won't come."

When they came to the river, Jim Winters was there, riding along on his pony. Of course, he wanted to see Patches do his trick. He was down from Bang's back in a minute.

Patches went after sticks until Billy saw that he was getting all tired out.

Then Jim climbed up on his pony's back, pulled on the lines, gave Bang a slap to make him stop eating grass, and started off for home.

After that Billy looked around for a good place to fish. There was an old boat tied to a pine tree at the edge of the river. It had a flat bottom and was a safe kind of boat for a boy to sit in. Someone must have used that boat not very long before because there were some oars in the bottom of the boat.

"Maybe we can get a fish," said Billy. He and Patches climbed into the boat.

But this was not Billy's lucky day. First he fished up an old shoe. Then a fat old turtle ate the worms, not once but five or six times.

Now and then, out in the middle of the river, a big fish would jump out of the water and fall back with a big splash.

"If we were out there," thought Billy, "we could catch a fish in a minute."

Just at that minute a bigger fish than ever jumped out of the water.

"Deep water is the place to fish," thought Billy. "And here I go!"

The rope that tied the boat to the tree was not fastened very well. Before many minutes the rope was in the boat.

Then Billy picked up the oars. He knew just what to do. Father had a boat of his own, and Billy had been out in it many, many times.

As soon as he was out in the middle of
the river, Billy put down the oars and
started to fish. All at once there was a
big pull on the fishline.

"I have him! I have him!" shouted
Billy. It was as much as he could do to
pull in that big fish. He was working so
hard that he did not see one oar as it
fell from the boat and was off down the
river, going faster every minute.

As soon as the fish was in the boat, Billy saw what had happened. Here he was out in the middle of the river with only one oar. Oh, how afraid he was!

Now Billy thought of something. It is surprising that he had not remembered it a long time before. Why had he come out in this boat? It wasn't his boat.

"Why, oh, why did I do it?" he thought. "I will keep on going away down the river. No one will see me and come to help me. I'm sure no one will. Maybe I won't stop until I am away out to sea. Maybe a big wave will wash over the boat. Oh, dear! I want my mother."

As the minutes flew by, Billy grew more afraid than ever.

All this time the oar was going down the river. Billy didn't even try to catch hold of it. It was too far away.

All at once Billy had a happy thought.

"Get the big stick, Patches. Get the big stick!" he cried, as he pointed to the oar.

In a minute Patches had jumped from the boat. He made his way through the water until at last he had the oar in his mouth. He had a hard, hard time getting back to the boat. Each minute it looked as if he could hold the oar no longer. But at last he made it.

How glad Billy was to get that oar. He started for the shore at once.

Patches knew that he could not climb back into the boat from the water. So he followed along by its side.

When Billy was almost to shore, he heard someone calling. It was Miss Lizzie.

As soon as Billy had left the garden, Miss Lizzie had been sorry about being so cross. So she had come down to the river to see the trick, after all. She got there just in time to see Patches as he came back with the oar. She was sure Billy would fall into the river.

"Oh, Billy! Get out of that boat! Oh, Patches, you good dog!" cried Miss Lizzie. Then she said the same words over and over. She was delighted when Billy was safe on shore once more.

And I tell you, Billy was happy, too. He tied the boat to the tree and never even thought of the fish.

Then Miss Lizzie, Billy, and Patches walked up the road to Billy's house.

Patches rested on the step while Miss Lizzie and Billy went into the house.

"Oh, Billy, Billy!" cried Mother, when she heard what had happened. "Why did you ever go out in that boat? You must never do that again. Never!"

And Billy was sure he would not.

"And now, where is that dog?" asked Mother. "Why isn't he here with you?"

"He is out on the steps, but he is all wet," said Billy.

"I don't care a thing about that," said Mother. "Bring him in! Bring him in!"

So Patches came into the house and had a good warm supper. And after that he stayed. He was Billy's dog in the daytime, and Miss Lizzie's dog at night. Mr. Carl laughed and called him the half-and-half dog.

So now if you go to Friendly Village and stop at Billy's house, you will find dog tracks on the steps and dog hair all over the floors. And Mother will tell you that Patches is a treasure, and she cannot see how she ever got along without him. As for Billy, he won't give you time to say "Hello!"

"Have you seen Patches?" he will say. "Patches is MY dog."

TWO KINDS OF LUCK

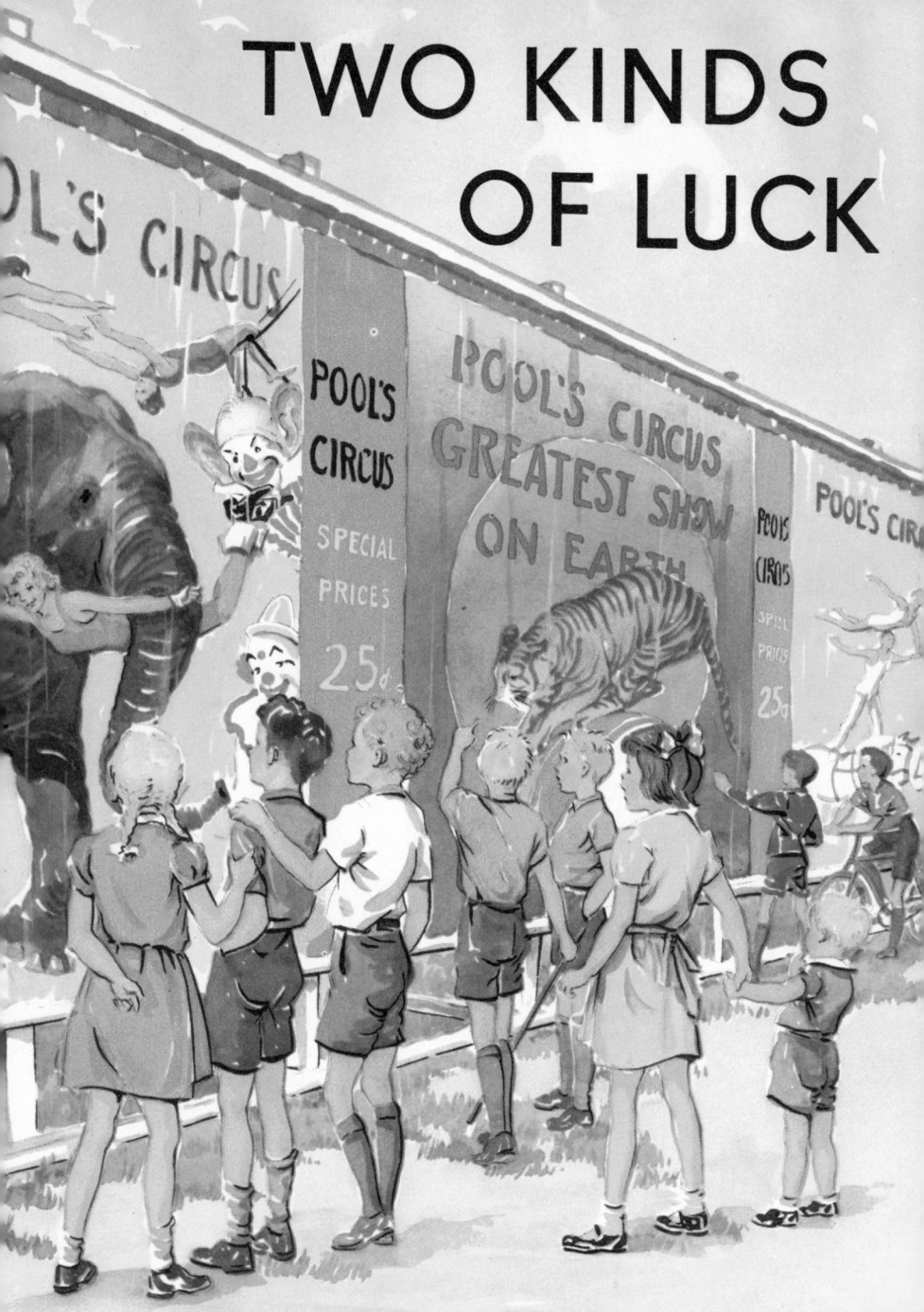

Bad Luck

There were three days of the year when Bobby Bell was never late for breakfast—Christmas, his birthday, and the day the circus came to town.

Today was not Christmas. Oh, my, no! It was a lovely day in summer. It was not Bobby's birthday. That came in May. So now if you are any kind of guesser, you know what day it really was.

Anyone going by Bobby's house about six o'clock in the morning might have seen Bobby open the back door. Then he brought in the milk for breakfast. The rest of the family were still in bed.

Bobby's eyes danced with fun. He was smiling to himself, a happy kind of smile. You could tell by his smile that he expected to have a good time.

His face was so clean that it looked like a shining red apple. His hands, his neck, and the back of his ears were just as clean. His hair was so smooth that not one hair was out of place. He didn't want anyone to send him back to clean up all over again. Not this morning!

The circus parade started at nine o'clock. Bobby wanted to be down on River Street long before that. He thought a circus parade was the grandest thing in the world. He wanted to be right out in front of all the people and see the parade from the minute it started.

Bobby could hardly wait to hear the music. He could hardly wait to see the animals and the big circus wagons. He could hardly wait to see the dancing clowns with paint all over their faces.

Bobby thought breakfast would never be ready. He was the first one to take his seat at the table. The minute he was seated, he began eating his fruit.

Then there was breakfast food. Mother had cooked that breakfast food just for him. It smelled very good as it steamed away on the table in front of him. He started to eat it. Then he stopped. It was good, but it was much too hot.

Bobby could not wait for the breakfast food to get colder. Not on this morning of all mornings, when the circus was coming to town!

Bobby was wishing as hard as he could
that he might get out of eating the rest
of his breakfast, when his sister, Martha,
made a discovery.

"Why, Bobby!" she said. "What is that
all over your face?"

"All over my face? Nothing!" said
Bobby. "I washed it in good hot water. It
is clean! I know it is! There can't be
anything on it!"

By this time Mother was looking at
Bobby, too.

"Oh, dear!" she said. "Your face is all covered with red spots. That is plain to be seen. Where in the world did they come from? Come here and let me look you over. I must send for the doctor right away."

Red spots! The doctor! That would mean bed. Bed! Think of going to bed on circus day, of all days! Bobby couldn't let that happen. He just couldn't!

"I feel fine, just fine," he cried. "I washed my face too hard. That is where the red spots came from. Please, Mother, please! Don't send for the doctor!"

But there was no stopping Mother.

The doctor lived only two doors away. He came in no time at all and gave one look at poor Bobby.

"Well, Mrs. Bell," he said. "This boy has the measles. The wisest thing to do is to put him to bed for a few days. Keep him very warm, and don't let him use his eyes."

"Oh, but I can't go to bed!" cried Bobby. "I feel fine, and I want to see the circus parade."

"That is too bad," said Doctor Lee. "I'm sorry, Bobby, but you will not see the circus parade this year. I must put a 'Measles' sign on your door, and you will have to stay in the house for two weeks. Be sure to keep very warm. Goodby! Better luck next year!"

Poor Bobby! What was the use of living if he missed the circus parade?

Mother put her arm around him. "I am sorry about the parade," she said. "But after all, you have seen it for the last two or three years, and circus parades are all alike. I hoped it was not the measles you had, but it is. When a boy has measles, he can't be running around. So you will have to go to bed. There is nothing else to be done about it."

"Did any boy ever have such bad luck as this?" thought Bobby, as he hopped into bed.

Mother covered him up, and then, to make him still warmer, she made a fire in the fireplace. Then she left him and went back to her work.

For a time Bobby watched the red fire. He had such a lonesome feeling. He longed—oh, how he longed—to be down on River Street watching the circus parade.

If only Martha could come to talk to him! She couldn't go to the parade, not with a "Measles" sign on the house. But she had to stay away from Bobby, too. She didn't want to catch the measles.

All at once Bobby thought that he heard music. But it was only the tweet, tweet of a bird and the wind in the branches of a tree near the window.

The clock ticked softly. The more it ticked, the more lonesome Bobby was. He couldn't stand it. He just couldn't!

"Better luck next year!" That is what Doctor Lee had said. Why, it would be a year before the circus parade came back to town!

A year had twelve months. Each month had four weeks. Each week had seven days. Right there Bobby stopped. He couldn't let himself think of all the days and weeks and months that must go by before the circus came again.

He was so hot that he was almost baked. He wanted to pull everything off the bed and stick his head out of the open window. But Mother had told him to be sure to keep covered up.

"I will cook if I stay here another minute," thought Bobby. "Just cook!"

Then he did something that he didn't want to do at all. He couldn't help it. You would have done the same thing if you had been there. He cried. But he crawled down under the blanket so that no one would know but himself.

I guess he cried until he grew sleepy. When Mother came back, she thought he was hiding under the blanket. But he was not hiding. He was fast asleep.

More Bad Luck

After circus day was over, staying in bed was not so bad. Mother thought nothing of leaving her work and spending her time with Bobby. When Father came home, he would do the same thing.

Bobby was forgetting about his bad luck when one day the postman brought letters from all the boys and girls. The letters didn't do much to help Bobby forget. They were full of news about the circus and the parade. But Bobby was glad to get them, anyway.

One day Bobby heard a tap outside the window. He looked up, and there were Alice and Jerry. Jerry was the one who had tapped. Alice couldn't tap. She was holding a big cake that Miss Lizzie had made for Bobby.

Then what a feast there was! Alice and Jerry stood outside the window and ate cake. Mother and Bobby sat inside and ate cake. Martha helped herself in the kitchen.

Another day Father went to the city. When he came back, he had a shining new hammer for Bobby. But best of all, he had a pocket full of pennies. He said that he would hide the money everywhere in the house. The first day Bobby was out of bed, he could get to work. He might have every penny he could find.

The first day Bobby found twenty pennies, the next day twenty-five. He went on looking until he found almost one hundred. By this time he was very proud of himself.

At last the two weeks were over, and I suppose you think that the bad luck was over, too. But it was not over, as you will see.

It was the morning when the doctor was supposed to come to take down the sign. This same morning Paddy's mother called up to see if Bobby could come to Paddy's birthday party that afternoon. She was going to take the boys and girls to a picture show. After that they were coming back to Paddy's house for ice cream and cake and other good things that you have at a party.

Mother said that Bobby could go if the doctor said so, and if the sign were down in time.

The doctor didn't come, and he didn't come. Mother called up his house. His wife said that he had been called to the city and would not be back before afternoon.

It was time to go to the party. Still no doctor! Poor Bobby! Did any boy ever have such bad luck as this?

Bobby watched the other boys and girls race down the street. He watched them as they got into the car. Then Paddy's mother drove them all away.

The minute they had gone, the doorbell started to ring. It was the doctor. Of course, he was sorry about being late, but that didn't help any. He took down the sign and told Bobby to put on his coat and cap and go out to play.

Out to play! There was no one to play with. Bobby sat down on the front steps with his head in his hands. He had all the bad luck in the world. And no one cared a thing about him! No one cared a dime!

He picked up a stick from the grass and began playing with it. What could a boy do all by himself? Of course, if he had a boat and some oars, he could go out upon the river and fish. He had always wanted to be a fisherman. But he didn't have a boat. He didn't even have a fishline. He wished he had a dog. A cross dog that would snap at everyone!

Now, of course, Bobby didn't really want a snapping dog. He just thought that because he was feeling so lonesome. Bad luck always makes you feel that way.

Luck Turns

After a while Bobby looked up at the blue sky and the white clouds. There was nothing else to look at. He stood up and leaned against the post.

All at once he remembered something. He knew someone who cared. He knew someone who would be sorry about his bad luck. He was going to find her right away.

The next minute he was trotting down Green Gate Road to find Miss Lizzie.

Miss Lizzie had been to Cobbler Jim's shop. She had left some shoes there to have the holes in the soles mended. She was coming home just as Bobby got to the green gate.

Miss Lizzie knew that Bobby had missed the circus, but she could not believe that he had missed Paddy's party, too. That was too much bad luck for any one boy.

"But that is the way sometimes," she said. "Bad luck and more bad luck! I know just how you feel. When I was a girl, there was nothing I liked so much as a circus. I remember one time when I didn't have money to buy a ticket, and I didn't know how to make any money. I cried for a week."

It made Bobby smile to think that Miss Lizzie had once been a girl who liked to go to a circus. There was something funny about that. He had always thought of Miss Lizzie as being grown-up.

"Were you really a girl, Miss Lizzie?" he asked. "What did you look like?"

"Oh, I was not bad-looking," said Miss Lizzie. "Maybe you would like to see my picture."

Before long Bobby and Miss Lizzie were sitting side by side on the garden seat. Miss Lizzie handed Bobby some pictures.

One picture showed Miss Lizzie when she was a girl. She was playing with some shells in the sand on the sea-shore, and the waves were rolling in.

There was another picture that showed a ship just ready to go to sea.

"I'm on that ship! There I am, right up in front!" said Miss Lizzie, as she pointed to a little girl in the picture.

Still another picture showed a mountain trail, and the cabin where Miss Lizzie used to live in the summertime.

Bobby and Miss Lizzie were having the best time together when all at once a car stopped outside the green gate.

"I declare! Found at last, Bobby, my boy! You might think I was a peddler the way I have gone from house to house looking for you," someone called.

Bobby looked up. There, looking in at them, was Uncle Andrew. Uncle Andy, as Mother called him, was so funny and kind that Bobby wished he would come a hundred times more than he did.

"Uncle Andrew! Uncle Andrew!" Bobby shouted at the top of his voice. "Oh, I am so glad to see you! I didn't know you were coming to our house."

"I didn't know it myself until this morning," said Uncle Andrew. "I didn't call you up because I wanted to surprise you.

"Now tell me," said Uncle Andrew, as he opened the gate and walked in. "Why are you and Miss Lizzie sitting here all alone on this lovely afternoon? Where are all the other boys and girls?"

By this time Bobby was jumping up and down. At last he was feeling happy.

"I have had the measles!" he cried. "And all the other boys and girls have gone to Paddy's party. I couldn't go because the doctor didn't take the sign down in time."

"Measles!" cried Uncle Andrew. "Why, Bobby! What a time of year to have the measles! If you had to have them, why didn't you tell them to come in the wintertime when you have to stay in the house anyway? Lovely summer days are no days for measles. And why didn't you send them away in time to go to the party?"

How Bobby laughed at Uncle Andrew!

"I don't care, now that you are here," said Bobby. "It was not so bad having the measles. Everyone was good to me. But I didn't see the circus. That is what I call bad luck."

"Circus! Don't tell me that you had the measles when the circus came to town," said Uncle Andrew.

Bobby had to say, "Yes." Even with Uncle Andrew around, he didn't feel happy about that. "Didn't even see the parade," he said with his head down.

"Well, of all things! What do you know about that?" said Uncle Andrew.

"I know just how he feels," said Miss Lizzie. "Old as I am, I like a circus. I would walk miles to see one this very minute."

"Now, don't tell me that you would walk miles, Miss Lizzie! Would you, really?" laughed Uncle Andrew.

Then a smile started in his eyes and around his mouth. Soon that smile covered his face.

"I believe I can do something about this," he said. "I really believe I can. May I go into your house, Miss Lizzie? I must call up someone right away."

"What do you suppose he is going to do?" asked Bobby, as he danced up and down and smiled all over. "Oh, Miss Lizzie, I can hardly wait."

"I'm sure I don't know what he is going to do," said Miss Lizzie. "All I can say is that it sounds like something pretty exciting."

In a minute or two, Uncle Andrew was back again.

"Hop into the car, the two of you," he said, "and not a question out of you. We are going somewhere. So keep quiet."

"What will Mother say?" asked Bobby.

"I told you—no questions. She knows all about it," said Uncle Andrew.

Miss Lizzie tried to say that she couldn't go. She just couldn't. But Uncle Andrew would not let her say it.

In the end Uncle Andrew had to wait while Miss Lizzie went into the house to get ready. When she joined them again, she was all dressed in blue. She didn't even have on her everyday hat. Oh, no! She had put on her best hat with the gay red roses.

Then into the car they stepped. Uncle Andrew stopped at the garage for gas. Then away they went. He stepped on the gas, and away they went. But where in the world do you think they were going?

On the Way to Good Luck

"Where are we going? Where are we going?" Bobby asked that question a hundred times or more as the car went flying down the road and out of town. Miss Lizzie asked the same question.

For a while, all Uncle Andrew would do was smile and say, "Oh, nowhere! Nowhere!" But when Bobby could stand it no longer, Uncle Andrew had to tell.

"Well, if you must know, we are going to a circus. Where else would I take you on a lovely summer day like this?"

"To a circus! What are you talking about?" cried Bobby.

"About a circus! I'm talking about a circus. We are going over to Watertown to see the circus," said Uncle Andrew.

"You mean that, Uncle Andrew?" cried Bobby. "You are not joking, are you?"

"Not joking at all," said Uncle Andrew. "I just happened to see some big circus pictures as I drove through Watertown. I happen to know Mr. Pool, the man who owns that circus, too. I called him up when I was in Miss Lizzie's house. I asked him what he was doing, bringing his circus to Friendly Village when you had the measles. He is a nice fellow. He was sorry you missed seeing his clowns and animals. He thought you might like to come over to Watertown to see them."

"Uncle Andrew," cried Bobby. "We will never get there in time! Half the afternoon is gone now. It is three o'clock."

"No, we won't get there in time," said Uncle Andrew. "And this afternoon is the last time the circus is showing. Mr. Pool told me that the circus has been in Watertown three days. It will be a long jump to the next stopping place. So the circus will be on the move as soon as this afternoon's show is over."

Talk about bad luck! This was going to be the hardest luck of all!

Just then Uncle Andrew smiled and whispered something to Miss Lizzie.

"Why, Bobby," he said then. "Who wants to see a circus? Miss Lizzie and you and I have seen a circus many, many times. Today we are going to see something better. And we won't even have to have a dollar to buy a ticket.

"We are going to see the circus people put the circus to bed, or whatever you call it," Uncle Andrew went on.

"We are going to see them take down the tents. We will see the animals, and maybe we will have supper with the clowns."

"You are not joking?" cried Bobby. "Say that you are not joking! Oh, Uncle Andrew, what a picnic we will have! No other boy in all the world has an uncle like you!"

"Well, now, come to think of it," chuckled Uncle Andrew, "you are right. When it comes to being an uncle, I take the prize. How about it, Miss Lizzie?"

And, of course, Miss Lizzie said, "Yes."

It was a good thing that Uncle Andrew and not Bobby was at the wheel of the car. They were going fast enough as it was. Once they went over a bump, and Miss Lizzie's hat with the gay red roses almost flew out of the car. Once they almost ran into an old brown mule.

Good Luck at Last

When Uncle Andrew drove up, the circus was over, and crowds of people were leaving "The Big Top." That is what the big circus tent is called. Bobby wished that he could call out and tell everyone the exciting things that were going to happen to him.

As soon as they got out of the car, a jolly-looking man came up to them.

"Hello, Andrew," he called. "Hello! Hello! My, but it is good to see you again. And is this the boy who had measles when the circus came to town?"

"Yes, this is Bobby," said Uncle Andrew. "And this is Miss Lizzie, who would walk miles just to see a circus."

How Mr. Pool laughed when he heard that! "Come right along," he called. "We haven't much time."

As they walked along, Bobby looked about him. Everywhere he looked, he saw people at work. There were so many of them that Miss Lizzie said they made her think of bees.

Men were running in and out of circus tents, taking off their red coats and queer hats as they went. A beautiful circus lady rode by on a white horse.

Some men were at work taking down the side-show tents. Other men fastened long runways to the backs of the circus trucks. Then up the long runways and into the trucks went the circus wagons and the animals.

Bobby wanted to stand and look and look, but Mr. Pool called, "Hurry along, Bobby. The boys will be taking down 'The Big Top' in just a few minutes."

When they walked into the big tent, everything was very still. "The Big Top" looked much, much bigger than when it was full of animals and people.

"Were there really three rings? Were they all full of clowns and animals and circus people doing their tricks at the same time?" asked Bobby.

"Yes, this is a real three-ring circus," said Mr. Pool. "See what you missed by having the measles?"

They walked on through "The Big Top" to another tent, and there Mr. Pool stopped.

"May we come in?" he called.

"Ting-a-ling! Ring the bell, bring me a big piece of pie, and sing me a song," called a funny little voice.

"I have no pie," laughed Mr. Pool, "and I can't sing a song. You know I can't."

"Can't sing a song? Why, I thought you were a bird. I thought you were a nightingale," said the funny little voice.

"Well, I am not," laughed Mr. Pool. "Come, let me in. There are a lady and a boy out here to see you."

"A lady and a boy! Is the lady good-looking? Can the boy stand on his head?" called the same voice.

Then out through the hole in the tent came a funny white face and an arm holding a candle. The eyes in the funny white face were not open. The candle moved up and down so that it was shining on the faces of Bobby and Miss Lizzie.

"I may be blind, but they look all right to me," said the voice. "Come in! Come in!"

Then what do you think Bobby saw inside that tent? There, seated on boxes, were two clowns.

One clown was tall, the tallest man Bobby had ever seen. He was just as skinny as he was tall. His ears were ten times as big as Bobby's, and there was a big red smile painted on his funny white face.

The other clown was not tall at all, and he was very, very fat. He was as fat as the first clown was skinny. He was taking off the two biggest shoes in all the world.

"We are twins. Handy is my name," said the tall skinny clown in his funny little voice.

"Yes, we are twins. Sandy is my name," said the fat clown in his big deep voice.

"Oh, I know you!" cried Bobby. "I saw you in the circus parade last year."

"Last year?" said Handy. "Why not this year?"

"Last year?" said Sandy. "Where were you this year?"

"I had measles on circus day," said Bobby. "That is why Mr. Pool told Uncle Andrew that I could come around now."

"Measles!" said Handy in his queer little voice. "What's this I hear? The boy had measles!" Then he began making such funny sounds that Bobby and Miss Lizzie laughed and laughed.

"Measles!" said Sandy in his big deep voice. "Red spots here, there, and everywhere. I had them myself one time. They made me look like this."

And then while Bobby laughed until his sides hurt, Sandy painted little red spots all over his funny white face.

Next Sandy leaned over to go on taking off his big shoes. While he was doing that, Handy painted a deer with antlers on top of Sandy's smooth white head. Bobby and Miss Lizzie laughed harder than ever.

Then that big tall clown leaned over, and right out of Sandy's suit he pulled a little pig. Even Uncle Andrew laughed when he saw that.

The poor pig ran around and around the tent until Sandy helped it back into the pocket in the side of his suit.

"Have you seen Dolly?" Handy asked next. "Poor Dolly! Poor old Doll!"

Out from behind some boxes came a dog. Was she a real dog? Bobby was not sure because she was so small.

"She must be the smallest dog in the world," thought Bobby.

Even the dog's bow-wow was small, but she could wag her tail faster than any other dog Bobby had ever seen. She was as black as black could be. Around her neck was a big red ribbon, and on the end of her tail was a big red feather.

"Here, Dolly! Here, old girl!" called Handy. He leaned over and fastened a little piece of rope around the dog's neck. The dog started to run around the tent, and Handy followed. He made believe that the dog was pulling him. Bobby was sure he had never seen anything so funny as the tall clown and the little dog.

"No fair! Stop that!" cried Sandy in a
deep, cross voice. "Dolly isn't funny.
Wait until you see my White-foot."

Sandy went over to the door of the tent. "Here, White-foot, old boy!" he called. "Come in here and bring your pipe and do some tricks for the lady."

In through the door of the tent came a brown goat with one white foot.

"Oh, that goat!" said Mr. Pool to Uncle Andrew. "He is up to more mischief than all the other circus animals put together. But there is no use talking about selling him. Once these clowns had a donkey called Mac. All he could do was hee-haw all over the place. But when I gave him away, Handy and Sandy almost left the circus. And they are the two best clowns I have. So when they say White-foot must stay, they always win out."

By this time Sandy had turned a pail upside down. White-foot was all dressed up in a red coat. On his head was a tall black hat. There he sat on the pail with his pipe in his mouth, his funny whiskers, and his horns sticking out of his hat. Bobby laughed until he cried.

"What next?" cried Bobby, when White-foot was through showing off and had run from the tent, calling, "Ma-a-a!"

"What next?" said Handy. "Why, the boy thinks we can go on forever. Don't you know that the show is over?"

"Don't tell me the boy didn't know that the show is over!" said Sandy. "I want my supper. I am a hungry clown, and I want some flapjacks and bacon."

And then do you know what happened? Sandy pulled one thing and then another out of his clown suit. The pig came, too. When Sandy was through and his suit was off, he was not fat at all. When he put on his street shoes, they were not much bigger than Bobby's.

As for Handy, he had two legs made out of wood fastened to his own two feet. When he used some pincers and took off the legs, he was no bigger than Sandy.

Then Handy took off the big ears. When the two clowns took off the covering from the tops of their funny white heads, Bobby saw that their hair was yellow.

By the time their funny white faces were cleaned and washed, Handy looked just like Sandy, and Sandy looked just like Handy. They really were twins. Even their funny voices were gone. They looked alike, and they talked alike. And no one would have guessed that they were two clowns in a circus.

Luck, and More Luck

When Miss Lizzie, Uncle Andrew, Mr. Pool, and Bobby left the clown tent, they went into another tent full of circus people. Everyone was hard at work, but everyone gave Bobby a big smile and said hello to Miss Lizzie.

Bobby walked around and looked at the red coats, the tall hats, and all the other things going into the big trunks. The trunks were long and flat. Most of them had been bumped in many, many places. Inside and outside they were all covered with pictures of clowns and circus animals. They were so full that not another thing would go in.

The fat lady of the circus sat by one of the trunks. Bobby stopped to help her. It was hard for her to pack her trunk. She was so very fat.

"She must like bracelets," thought Bobby. She had ten on one fat arm. In one of them was a sky-blue turquoise.

I couldn't tell you all the things Bobby and Miss Lizzie saw after that. They called on the circus lady with the beautiful white horse, and Bobby had a ride. Not a long ride, but a ride just the same! They saw a dog that could play the fiddle, and what a fiddler he was! They saw all the animals there were to see. They watched as the trucks carried the last of the circus animals away.

The animals Bobby liked best were the monkeys. My, but they liked to show off! They pulled one another's tails and played all kinds of tricks. Bobby laughed to see them run after one another all over the big circus cage.

One monkey shook hands with Bobby and played a trick at the same time.

"Watch out!" called Mr. Pool, but he was too late. Something sticky was all over the monkey's hand, and Bobby could hardly get his own hand away.

After that Mr. Pool took them into the long cook tent for supper. Bobby had never seen so much food. He had never seen such long tables. Circus people came and went. Everyone ate in a hurry because there was much work to be done.

While Bobby was eating, a big truck backed right up to the tent door. Men began to put pots and pans, jugs and boxes and dishes into that big truck.

Bobby was never sure what he had for supper that night. Maybe he had some potatoes and a few things like that. But the only thing he was sure of was the pie. I will tell you why.

All at once Handy and Sandy came walking in and sat down at Bobby's table. Each of them had a big pie.

"Here we are again," they called. "We are feasting on pie tonight."

Now Bobby knew what he wanted—pie!

"My pie is full of apples. Will you have some?" asked Handy.

"My pie is full of bananas. Will you have some?" asked Sandy.

Handy gave Bobby a piece of pie, and Sandy gave him another. So now you know why Bobby remembered the pie.

And then came the big surprise. Bobby always said that it was better than any Christmas or birthday surprise he had ever had.

Handy got up from the table and looked at Miss Lizzie. He stood there with his hands behind him.

"Show me the hand you want," he said. Miss Lizzie pointed to the left hand.

Then Handy gave Miss Lizzie a picture, and he gave Bobby another. They were pictures of Handy and Sandy in their clown suits. At the bottom of Bobby's picture were the words, "From Handy and Sandy to the boy who had measles on circus day." On Miss Lizzie's picture were the words, "To the lady who is as nice as our granny and our Aunt Betsy."

What surprise could be better? When Bobby saw the picture, he was so happy that he just stood and looked at it. He was too happy to say, "Thank you," and so Miss Lizzie said it for him.

Then Miss Lizzie and Uncle Andrew and Bobby walked out to the car that was to carry the clowns and Mr. Pool away.

"I will be right down on the front seat when the circus comes to town next year," called Bobby, as the car started away.

"Don't let the doctor get you," said Handy in his funny clown voice. Then he made a funny face at Bobby.

"Come back next year, and I will show you how to be a clown," called Sandy in his deep clown voice. Then he made a funny face, too.

Bobby and Miss Lizzie waved and waved until they could see the car no longer.

It was long after sundown when the last truck started on its way. Miss Lizzie, Uncle Andrew, and Bobby stayed until the very end.

"There goes the circus until next year," said Bobby, as at last they turned away.

The moon was coming up as Uncle Andrew started the car on its way home. Bobby was too tired to talk. He just sat in the seat, proudly holding the picture.

"How much will you take for that picture?" Uncle Andrew asked with a smile.

"I'm not trading this picture for anything," said Bobby. "Not for anything in the world."

Just as they crossed the tracks into Friendly Village, Bobby looked at Uncle Andrew.

"Don't go home again! Ever!" he said.

As Uncle Andrew smiled, Bobby went on. "Did you ever know a boy to have such bad luck and good luck all in two weeks?"

"No," chuckled Uncle Andrew. "I didn't. And the best thing is that the good luck followed the bad."

Acknowledgments

Special acknowledgment is accorded the following authors who generously furnished textbook rights on original stories from which ideas were taken and adaptations were made:

Lavinia R. Davis for *Patsy Trains for Jack's Rodeo* adapted into the story of "Bang."

Olive Beeman for *Turkey Tails* adapted into a portion of the story of "Patches."

Margaret Friskey for *A Little Fisherman's Luck* adapted into the last portion of the story of "Patches."

Renee Buhlman for *Tommy Todd's Two Kinds of Luck* adapted into the story "Two Kinds of Luck."

Word List

This book is designed to develop reading readiness on the third year level. The following list includes the words in *The New Through the Green Gate* not taught in preceding books of the series. All these words are introduced again and are retaught in the basic Third Reader, *The New If I Were Going*.

5 Lizzie	19-22	79-95	135 measles
6	23 slap	96 turkey	136-139
7 chimneys	24 across	97-107	140 months
wall	25	108 teach	141-166
8 yellow	26 arm	109-116	167 men
9 hat	27-37	117 bottom	168
roses	38 against	oars	169 pie
10	lines	118-122	170
11 Amber	39-40	123 pointed	171 tall
12	41 whistle	124-127	172-175
13 fall	42-71	128 half	176 small
14	72 nine	129	177
15 Bang	73-75	130 Christmas	178 pipe
16 brother	76 tracks	131 paint	179-181
17	77 wags	132	182 trunks
18 skinny	78 bicycle	133 sister	183-191
hundred		134 doctor	